The Original Story of the Tooth Fairy

The Beginning of a Legend

Lance Douglas

Snow Canyon Publishing

There once lived a handsome King and a beautiful Queen who were dearly loved by the people of their kingdom. The King and Queen were always warmly greeted by the people as their royal coach traveled throughout the kingdom.

Outside of the King and Queen's castle gate was the royal garden. In the royal garden lived a quiet little mouse. At night, while everyone in the kingdom was sleeping, the mouse loved to feast on the fresh fruits and vegetables in the garden.

The little mouse was so happy in the royal garden! However, she wondered what it would be like to live in the castle and be the royal mouse. One night, when the moon was full and bright, the little mouse quietly scampered under the castle gate, across the royal cobblestones, up the royal rainspout and into a moonlit room.

As the little mouse quietly made her way into the room and climbed to the top of the royal clock, the light of the moon softly showered its rays through the window. At first the little mouse could not believe her eyes. She looked once, then twice, and then a third time to be sure. It was a little boy and girl peacefully sleeping in their beds!

The little mouse never knew that the King and Queen had children. She had heard playful sounds coming from inside the castle walls. She had always been curious what those sounds were. But now she knew; it was the royal children!

Day after day the little mouse would quietly watch the royal children play in their room. She wanted so much to be their friend, but she knew that children of the King and Queen could never be friends with a mouse.

One day the little mouse heard the Princess cry out, "Mommy, my tooth has fallen out!"
The Queen quickly came running.

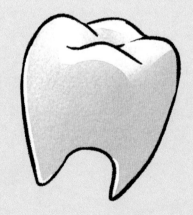

The Princess had always wondered what it would be like to lose a tooth. It felt so strange! There was a hole in her mouth and she could not stop looking at it in the mirror.

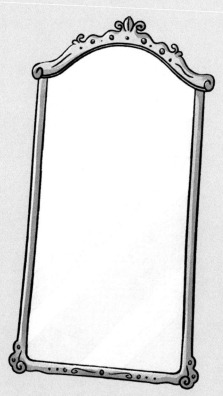

The young Princess asked her mother, the Queen, if she could sleep with her tooth.

"Your tooth will get lost if you sleep with it." the Queen warned.

But the Princess had a brilliant idea!

"I will place the tooth under my pillow to keep it safe?" she explained.

That night the little mouse watched intently as the royal children fell asleep. Then, without even thinking, the little mouse scampered across the floor, up the bedpost and under the pillow of the sleeping Princess. There it was, the shiny, white tooth of the Princess! The mouse could not believe her eyes. She had never seen a tooth before.

 The curious mouse held up the tooth into the glistening light of the moon. It was so beautiful! Suddenly a magical moonbeam came shooting through the window landing on the mouse and the tooth. The moonbeam instantly turned the mouse into a sparkling fairy and the tooth into a shooting star. The mouse, who had now become a fairy, watched in amazement as the tooth became a shooting star and found its place among the other stars in the night sky.

"Oh no! The tooth is gone! What shall I do?" cried the fairy.
Then the fairy had a brilliant idea. She could replace the tooth with a little treasure. When the Princess would wake up in the morning she would see that her tooth had been replaced with a small treasure. She would be so happy!

The fairy watched anxiously as the morning sunlight slowly filled the room of the royal children. Suddenly the Princess shouted with excitement, "My tooth is gone, but it has been replaced with a treasure!"
The children danced with joy as the fairy watched happily from the window.

News spread quickly about the Princess' lost tooth and her treasure. Soon all of the children throughout the kingdom would place their lost teeth under their pillows at night. Every night the little fairy would search the entire kingdom for children who had lost a tooth. Each lost tooth would be replaced with a small gift, and another bright star would be added to the night sky.

Now, many years later, news of
the tooth fairy has spread to
children all around the world.
Every night a child's lost tooth is
replaced by a gift or a small
treasure, and another beautiful star
is magically added to the night sky.

Dedicated to Brooklyn,
my little Princess.

Made in the USA
Monee, IL
27 April 2021